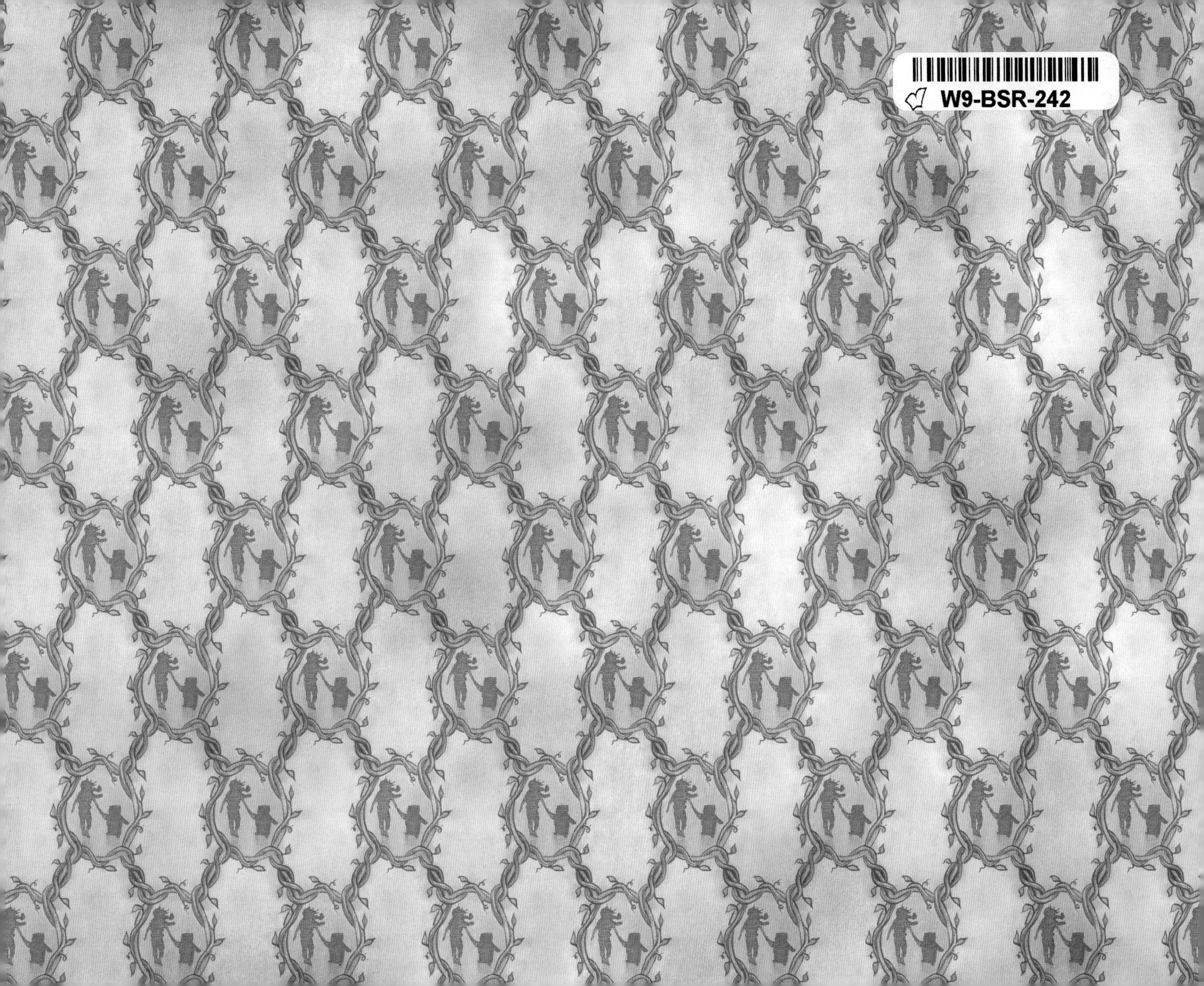

For my beautiful wife, Molly

Henry Holt and Company, *Publishers since 1866*
Henry Holt® is a registered trademark of Macmillan Publishing Group, LLC
175 Fifth Avenue, New York, NY 10010 • mackids.com

Library of Congress Control Number: 2017957761
ISBN 978-1-250-12748-8

Our books may be purchased in bulk for promotional, educational, or business use.
Please contact your local bookseller or the Macmillan Corporate and Premium Sales Department at
(800) 221-7945 ext. 5442 or by e-mail at MacmillanSpecialMarkets@macmillan.com.

First edition, 2018 / Designed by Patrick Collins
The artist used watercolor with pen and ink on Arches Hot Press Watercolor Board,
and added color digitally to create the illustrations for this book.
Printed in China by RR Donnelley Asia Printing Solutions Ltd.,
Dongguan City, Guangdong Province

1 3 5 7 9 10 8 6 4 2

A Hoot & Olive Story

Brave Enough for Two

Jonathan D. Voss

Henry Holt and Company
New York

Hoot was Olive's very best friend in the whole wide world. But as you know, best friends don't always like the same things. Take, for example, adventures. Olive preferred the kind found in books. Hoot, on the other hand—well, he preferred something a little different.

One day Hoot said, "I've made something special for you. But it could be a small bit scary and a slightly bigger bit adventurous."

"You know I don't like adventures," said Olive, "I'm not brave like you."

"Don't worry," said Hoot. "I will be brave enough for both of us."

"It's very nice," said Olive.

"Does it go high?"

"A little," said Hoot, climbing
into the basket. "But not too high."
Olive followed after.

Up they rose, over
rooftops and treetops till
the ground looked like
a giant patchwork quilt
passing beneath them.

"What do you think?"
asked Hoot.

"I think this is what it's
like to be a cloud," said Olive.
"But we've gone way more than
a little high."

Just then, a drop of water
landed on her nose.

The clouds darkened and thunder cracked with a flash of light. Giant drops poured from the sky. The wind swirled. The basket rocked.

"What if the wind blows us far away and we get lost?" cried Olive.

Hoot squeezed her hand. "We can never be lost," he said, "so long as I'm here and you're there, and here and there aren't very far apart."

All of a sudden, the sun poked through the clouds. The wind calmed.

"Look," said Hoot. "A rainbow."

Olive smiled.

Hoot untied the balloons one by one.
Lower and lower the basket dropped . . .

. . . till it scraped the ground
and toppled over.

The pair rolled out,
head over bottom,
into a patch of grass.

"We made it!" said Olive in a surprised
sort of way. "What should we do now?"
"Of course we made it," said Hoot.
"And now . . . I have another idea."

Hoot pushed the basket into a nearby river.

"I've never been in a boat before," said Olive.

"Then it will be the first time for both of us," said Hoot.

"Will we go fast?" asked Olive.

"Maybe just a little," said Hoot, tying a flag to their new ship's mast.

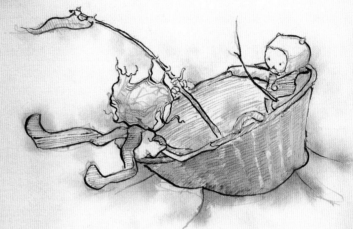

The boat bobbed and spun like a carnival ride.

"What do you think?" asked Hoot.

"I think we are going faster than just a little!" said Olive.

Down the river they sped till
it became a bubbling cauldron of
rocks and waves.

"We're going way too fast!"
cried Olive.

Hoot paddled with all his might.
"Don't be afraid!" he said. "I'll keep
you safe!"

And he did.

But on the shore, Hoot stood silent.

"What's the matter?" asked Olive.

Hoot picked up a piece of his stuffing.

"I'm not feeling all that well."

Olive paused—but only for a moment.
Then she said, "Don't worry, Hoot. I'll lead
the way home. I will be brave enough for
both of us."

Hoot followed her every step.

"It will be dark soon," he said.
"If it gets dark, we might get lost."

"Hoot," said Olive in a kind
way, "so long as I'm here and
you're there, and here and there
aren't very far apart, we can never
be lost."

Just as the sun began to set, a familiar
sight appeared.

"Home!" said Olive and Hoot together.

That night, Hoot got a patch.
"For bravery," said Olive. "And
tomorrow, how about I choose the
adventure?"

Hoot smiled.

"I was afraid today," he said, "when my stuffing
came out. But you were brave. And you kept me safe."
"Don't ever be afraid," Olive whispered. "I'll always
keep you safe."

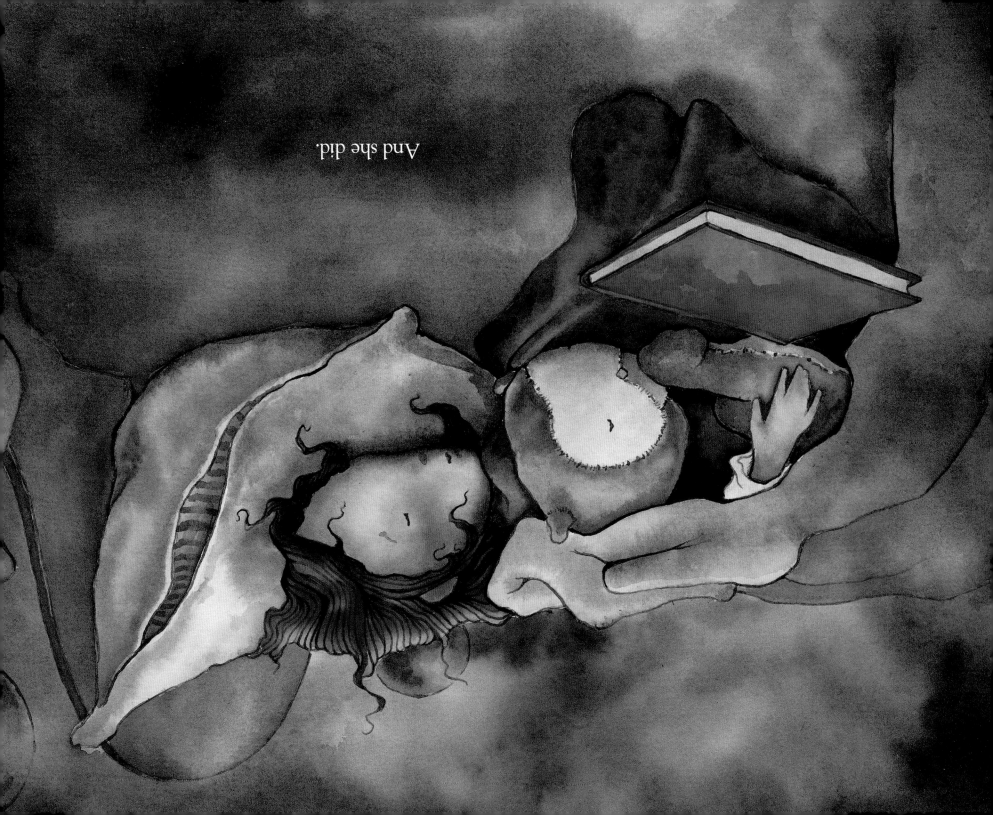

And she did.